W9-DIW-531

DISCARDED

JULY 2010
Bayport Public Library
Bayport, MN 55003

Ice Cream
at the
Castle

Written by Ann Love

Beautifully illustrated by Toni Goffe

The author's royalties are donated to cancer research.

Published by Child's Play (International) Limited
Swindon   Auburn ME   Sydney   St Catharines
© Ann Love 1999   Printed in Singapore
ISBN 0-85953-678-5 (soft cover)
ISBN 0-85953-677-7 (hard cover)
A catalogue reference for this book is available from the British Library.

One morning, the royal family exercises
were interrupted by Sir Percy, the palace purser.

Averting his gaze from the perfectly formed royal frames,
Sir Percy prized open the royal purse.

"Sire," he announced.
"I have news… some good and some dire, Sire…"

"What is the bad news?"
puffed kind King Clifford.

"Your royal purse is empty, Sire.
There is no money left … You are skint!"

"Then what is the good news?"
gasped the king.

"I am about to leave on my annual holiday cruise,"
replied the purser.

"Does that mean we won't be able to afford any more school lessons?" asked Prince Paul, hopefully.

"No! It means, your allowance will be reduced!" replied Sir Percy. "And everybody else's."

"What! Even mine?" shrieked King Clifford, the queen and the queen mother in unison.
"This is a disaster! Please, dear Sir Percy, tell us how we can raise money!"

"There is one thing…" Sir Percy began.

"What is it? they howled. "Tell us! We'll do ANYTHING! Except work, of course!"

"Well," continued the purser, "we could try taxes..."

"How would that help?" cried the queen.
"Our horse and carriage are much cheaper than taxis."

"Not taxis, Ma'am. I mean a tax on the peasants! A TAX!"

The Captain of the Guard was passing by the open window. He overheard Sir Percy's last words.

"Attacks? Attacks?" he repeated. "Oh, no! We're being attacked!"

He ran as fast as he could to the battlements.

"Man the guns, men! That ruthless, rotten ruffian, King Rudolf, is sending his troops to attack us!"

The soldiers manned the battlements, guns at the ready, and waited ...and waited ...and waited.

When, at last, the penny dropped, everyone in the castle began to worry about paying taxes or losing their jobs.

Meanwhile, Prince Paul had arranged to have a picnic with his friends, Prince Peter and Princess Eleanor, in the valley which lay between the two kingdoms.

"Oh, dear! You don't look very happy today," said Princess Eleanor. "Whatever is the matter?"

Prince Paul told his friends about the problem with his allowance and as they ate, they thought.

"I know," suggested Princess Eleanor, at last. "Why don't you open your castle to the public and charge people to go in?"

Prince Paul leapt into the air for joy.

"What a great idea! Let's go and tell my father! Even better, let's make the arrangements ourselves."

When they reached the castle, they ran straight
to the kitchen. The cook was crying into the soup
she was preparing for dinner. Dr Potamus,
Prince Paul's tutor, was trying to cheer her up.

When she heard their plan, the cook brightened up.

"I could make snacks to sell to the visitors," she said.
"But what? All I've got to cook with is bones."

"It isn't as bad as all that," said Doctor Potamus.

"We still have milk from the dairy and fresh fruit from the orchard. And there is plenty of snow and ice in the mountains. I am sure I have just the recipe in my ancient Persian cookbook to make this idea work."

When the gong didn't sound for dinner, King Clifford
went down to the royal kitchen, where he found
Dr Potamus with three very happy children.

"Where is my dinner?" bawled the king. "I'm starving!"
"We've been waiting and waiting and waiting."

"Well, your Majesty," replied the tutor.
"Cook has made soup with old bones
...or there's snow cream, my new invention."

"What do you mean, there's no cream?"
asked the king, taking his first lick.
"This is a *nice* cream. Give me some more."

"You are right, Sire, as always," wheezed the tutor.
"Ice cream is a much better name."

After he had eaten his fill, the king was in a good mood.
He thought Princess Eleanor's idea of opening the castle
to paying visitors was a very good one.

"When they hear about my ice cream," announced the king, "visitors will flock to the castle. We will send out messengers far and wide. But we must keep it secret from King Rudolf. We don't want competition on our doorstep!"

"But how will people find their way?" asked Prince Paul. "We'll have to give them directions."

King Clifford agreed.

"That's why I have a royal chart-maker. Now he will have a chance to display his skill."

"This is a supreme example of my craft!"
boasted the royal chart-maker a little while later.

The children thought they could have done better.

"Maps have to be very clear for grown-ups to follow,"
said Prince Paul. "My father is always losing his way."

"But it will be all right, if we put enough of them
in the right places," said Princess Eleanor.

As the big day approached,
the cook and the tutor worked feverishly
to prepare a ton of ice cream.

The queen mother and her cats
played their part, too, testing the results.

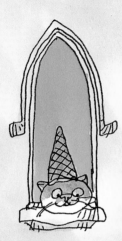
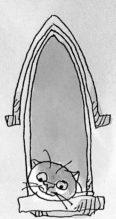

When the royal printer finished producing the maps, the king handed them to the Captain of the Guard.

"Tell your men to paste them on all the trees!" he commanded.

The children were upset.
The maps had been their idea.
Pasting them on the trees was another job
they had looked forward to.

The day and the hour arrived. The sun shone.
King Clifford, the queen, the queen mother and her cats,
the princes, Princess Eleanor and the royal household
waited …and waited …and waited.

But the expected visitors did not arrive.

The ice cream began to melt.

"Let's go and see my grandmother," suggested Prince Peter.
"She is bound to know what the problem is."

Prince Paul and Princess Eleanor agreed.
Prince Peter's grandmother really was extremely wise.

As they crossed the valley, the children saw hordes
of people making their way to the castle of King Rudolf.

"Something very odd is going on,"
said Prince Peter.
"But I just can't figure it out.
Can you?"

Meanwhile, inside King Rudolf's castle, unexpected visitors were pressing money into the perplexed king's palm.

"Is this the revolution?" he wondered uneasily.
"I thought revolutionaries looted, not gave money away!"

Everything in the castle seemed to interest the visitors.
But, in spite of their good-nature, King Rudolf
wished he hadn't given his guards the day off.

Suddenly, the mood changed. As Prince Paul and Prince Peter and Princess Eleanor arrived, an impatient voice was heard:

"We've paid our money. We've seen the sights.
Now, where's the ice cream?"

"Ice cream! Ice cream! Ice cream!" chanted the angry mob.

"I'll scream, too!" promised the king, screaming at the top of his voice to prove it. "I'll do anything you want."

Quickly and bravely,
the children came
to the rescue
of good King Rudolf.

"Ladies and gentlemen,"
they urged the visitors.
"Kindly, follow us
to the battlements!"

"You are at the wrong castle," smiled Prince Paul.
"Over there, look! That's where the ice cream is!"

Shrugging their shoulders, the visitors set off doggedly across the valley.

"You had better come, too, Uncle Rudolf!"
said Princess Eleanor.
"You will like ice cream. Everybody does."

"Clifford, old chum,"
promised King Rudolf, an hour or so later.
"Give me some more ice cream
and I will give you this sack of lovely money!"

And so, King Clifford's financial crisis was solved.

With a little help from the visitors, the ice cream
was saved from melting. For a while,
all the grown-ups were happy at the same time.

The children were happy, too. Their plan had worked.
But still they wondered why the visitors had gone
to the wrong castle.

The next morning, Prince Paul, Prince Peter
and Princess Eleanor took a closer look
at the maps on the trees.

Then, they understood that this is a topsy turvy world.

Maps do not always help us find our way.
Money problems have toppled kingdoms before and since.
But no one has ever been disappointed by ice cream.